ThE AmBIT

By

Kavita Passi Bisht

Clever Fox
PUBLISHING

Chennai • Bangalore

CLEVER FOX PUBLISHING
Chennai, India

Published by CLEVER FOX PUBLISHING 2023
Copyright © Kavita Passi Bisht 2023

All Rights Reserved.
ISBN: 978-93-56483-10-1

CONTENTS

A big Thanks to all my family and friends for their prayers and good wishes.

Gratitude to my loving Husband, my daughter, my sisters, mother and my in laws.

In the loving memory of my cousin, angel and Saviour Major Maina Sekhri.

FOREWARD

LIFE :

Well, Its not about how much I have lived, it is about how much I have learned about life, and here I am, to share my understanding of life.

Life is a mystery ......

it takes sadness to know happiness,

restlenesss to understand relief,

noise to appreciate peace and

absence to value presence

People say we live only once , but I believe that we can live every single moment of our life , only if we want to.

Life goes on, and takes you along too, through the ups and downs .

Sometimes life doesn't give you what you desire from it , not because you don't deserve it, but because you deserve better.

When life shows you the reasons to be sad , show it that you have reasons to smile . When you can't find the reason to your happiness, let yourself be the reason.

Let happiness become the goal of your life.

Life will go on , and will take you along too, and its you , and only you , who has to make a clear choice.

So , here I am ,

Wishing you a HAPPY LIFE

Kavita

CHAPTER 1

From Birth to Second Birth

"Life is a song Sing it.

Life is a game — Play it.

Life is a challenge — Meet it

Life is a dream — Realize it.

Life is a sacrifice — Offer it.

Life is love — Enjoy it" .... **Sai Baba**

Life is not as easy as we think it to be, day to day chores and routine is something which makes it move in one specified direction. We live in the same groove for years together, cribbing, complaining ,crying , laughing ,fighting etc till the time it gets hit with some small or major disaster

It changes completely when something miserable happens to oneself , yessss only when it is to SELF.....

There are many things which happen in the daily life — things going wrong, accidents, fights , office politics, home politics, disagreements and arguments with friends / colleagues / neighbors /anyone , demise of the near and dear ones leading to depression , sadness , anxiety but the person is most affected when something happens to oneself and where one has to fight for it , without knowing the consequences......

"The world comes to an end" would not be the right thing to mention nor can I say that it actually does because things go on and move on, but yes ofcourse it comes to halt , or to put it in the right way things go BLANK..... completely BLANK, similar to the ECG machine in the hospital which shows merely straight lines 〜〜 〜〜 〜〜 〜〜 〜〜 〜〜 〜〜 〜〜 〜〜 〜〜 〜〜 〜〜 when a person loses breath.

And so it started for me ....

An evening which was dark enough ,not only for me but also for all my buddies and close ones .... I could not understand, what would be the next step or what is going to happen the next moment, could not feel the presence of my infant, my husband, my mom , no body.................

I WAS COMPLETELY BLANK....

"Nothing in Life is to be feared , it is only to be understood . Now it is time to understand more , so that we may fear less ".

Marie Curie

Chapter 2

Unforseen Whammy

Life in its own pace was moving gradually, Morning blues , getting ready with the little one , dropping little one to the bus stop , rushing from home to office and back from office to home and plenty of other tits and bits in between before I use to hit the bed as late as by 11 in the night to again get up by 6 next morning .

"You can really only enjoy life when you are extremely busy"

Josephine de La Baume

In all this mish mash, one day it was noticed by my husband* that there was a big purplish black mark on one of my leg near the knee....so big that it was noticed, looked similar to any injury/wound mark* which went unnoticed by me, mainly because it was little above the calf muscle and below the knee. I was very casual when he asked and I just said that it would have been due to some hit by the table corner.

Who knew it would be a cause of my death or may be my nonexistence in this beautiful world.(till the time the person goes through any unforeseen thing the world doesn't seem to be beautiful)

In no time, may be a week or ten days similar black marks of different sizes appeared on both the legs and few on my hand. Considering it to be some skin infection or may be a side effect of food as diagnosed by one of the doctors, it still left me a bit worried. To be on the safer side and not be in a state of being sorry latter , I visited another doctor near my

---

*Bruise : blue mark after an injury.
* Mr. R Kapoor.   3

home. She was also of the same opinion that it might be a skin infection, but the good part was that she recommended few tests (which actually was a boon for me) without wasting a single day I went for the test and the day was May 1, 2011.

By evening the reports were in my hand and contradicting to my thoughts it was all messed up (though we could not conclude ,but many parameter were too high or too low) definitely being a cause of concern.

Negative thoughts protruding one after the other, I started thinking that it could lead to a never ending story of pain or maybe a start of journey of pain or a short story which would end in with an addition of "Late" in front of my name.

"When I have these negative thoughts and feelings , I like to dig into them because I like to get under them and see what's in there ."

Baron Vaughn

May 1, 2011 happened to be a Sunday and hence there were no specialist doctors available, had no choice but to wait for the next morning. Well as there is a saying "Rab Rakha[1]", something /some energy made me call my cousin Ms.Maina (we lost her in 2012—which was a huge loss/shock for the entire family).

When I narrated my report to her (which showed high WBC^2, low platelets, low hemoglobin) she was dumb stuck and wanted me to visit a Hematologist the very next day. I would not feel shy in telling you that, I wasn't even aware of as who a Hematologist[3] is ☺. For me she was my saviour, an angel sent by GOD to give me another birth.

---

1. Rab Rakha — God saves u.
2. WBC — White Blood Cells.
3. Hematologist — A specialist for blood related diseases.

That night was very long and the darkest of all for me and my husband. In this world of technology , google is the resort of every information and so I GOOGLED ☺ "black spots/marks on the body" and the first and most common result had the big word "CANCER" in it — something which no one would want to be diagnosed with. Though we were not aware of what had gone wrong or to put it right what is there in store for me in future, we were trying to be very positive and ruled out this word from our dictionary. Don't know whether my husband had really ruled it out from his thoughts but it was continuously knocking my thoughts 'CANCER ,CANCER,CANCER'.

No, No, No, No..........Uff what if it is there

"Human Spirit is the ability to face the uncertainty of the future with curiorsity and optimism . It is the belief that prblems can be solved , differences resolved . It is a type of confidence . And it is fragile . It can be blackened by fear and superstition."

Bernard Beckett

May 2, 2011, the deadliest day in my life ....

Me and my husband went to the nearby hospital with my haphazard reports and asked for a Hematologist, we were guided to a chamber where the placard read as "Dr. Bharat Vaswani" Hematologist and Oncologist—and reading the word "Oncologist" gave us shivers, but we had no choice but to wait for our turn to meet the doctor. Being a busy Monday morning the number of patients was high and by the time our turn came we had already waited for almost 2 hours.

My name was called and with trembling legs,

increased heartbeats, almost in a state of numbness, in a state of confusion, fear, and in desolation we showed the report to the doctor .

As he held the report in his hand was checking each parameters one by one like the WBC, hemoglobin, Platelets etc. and encircling each parameter , I literally felt that my heartbeat is gonna stop any time . After checking the reports he spoke and it did not even take minute for him to declare that I was suffering from cancer. He mentioned that although the report indicates that it is cancer but he would of course do a recheck

He said - "Its CANCER , Blood Cancer" and took the typical medical terminology Acute Promyelocytic Leukemia which is as difficult to understand as a foreign language , but yes he added that once the stage is detected with further tests , we would be in a better position to start the treatment and also that the if its in the initial stage it is completely curable .

"As a medical doctor, it is my duty to evaluate the situation with as much as I can gather and as much expertise as I have and as much experience I have to determine whether or not the wish of the patient is medically justified ."

Jack Kevorkian

The state of me and my husband was unimaginable — our feet and hands were almost numb and cold, tears were rolling down my cheeks, my husband sat speechless, though the doctor was saying that it is curable but we were unable to hear his words. A complete state of darkness was in front of our eyes.

Since I was completely shattered, my husband behaved to be strong, the doctor recommended few more tests – Bone marrow test being one of them. Long time back I had an uncle who had undergone a similar test and I had also read a lot about the test , so I knew it would be very painful. I did not want to undergo the same. As I mentioned Mr. Kapoor showed that he was strong enough, so he asked to go for the test .I had no choice, but yeah as I had read and heard the test was indeed very painful.

Test was done and, it was painful to the core. I wasn't in a state to walk and was taken in the wheel chair till the car. At home we couldn't talk and express much as my mom and my little one could not understand the pain.

The reports were to be collected in the evening and we had to meet the doctor with the reports. Probably my husband didn't wanted me to undergo a similar state in which I was in the morning, and also may be because he wanted to first calm himself and then me , hence himself went to collect the report. After a long wait when I called him, he said he is on the way back, but sounded sad and depressed. And that left me worried again.

I waited for him, and every second was so long. At home , my mom who was 70 plus, with whom I could not share my feelings, my little daughter who was merely 3 years, again with whom I could not share my feelings. I just hugged my little daughter and cried out my heart..... may be the feeling that I would not be there with her for long.☹

Finally the doorbell rings, and I could see him standing, trying to be calm and composed but I know it was very difficult for him to be calm. I could read his red swollen eyes which narrated the entire story .We went to the terrace, as probably he thought that after sharing the news he wouldn't be able to control or may be, I would lose my composure and act crazy .Ofcourse to avoid the entire scene in front of my mom and an infant my daughter.

My heart beats were very fast , I had crazy things jumping in my stomach, with my steps becoming so heavy that it refused to take a step forward ,somehow we reached the terrace which was a floor above my flat. And he started telling me, not directly coming to the point but finally revealed that I was now a patient - a "CANCER PATIENT "

"The art of medicine consists in amusing the patient while nature cures the disease."

Voltaire

---

*Names Changed

Chapter 3

Reality Acquainted

The evening had become darker for me with no hope of a new day with bright sunlight, though we were standing below the open sky, with cool breeze around but it had never felt so suffocated. Couldn't respond, was totally dumb stricken, the whole body was freezing. One wish if I was granted at that moment, I would have just changed the last minute....Of course nobody wants anything to happen to them at this age...at the age of just 32, rather I should at any age.

His first words still echo my ears " we need to fight it out, and we will leave all these things behind.... we will grow old together " and we hugged each other tightly, yeah with heavy heart and wet eyes .

"LIFE IS NOT A PROBLEM TO BE SOLVED , BUT A REALITY TO BE EXPERIENCED."

Soren Kierkegaard

And then it all started — phone calls to my dear ones to share a news no one had ever dreamt of even in their wildest dream. Mr. Kapoor on the other hand went for second and third opinion along with his friend Venkateshwar.

The first call I made was to my sister, my lifeline, my dearest friend who has been a mother to me, as she is almost 10 years elder to me. Unaware that she was in a party I just told her that, "di the reports have come and the doctor says I am suffering from cancer". Of course it was a shock for her and she was also speechless and the only thing she said was" I am coming tomorrow " Latter she told me that ,the moment she heard this news she couldn't control her tears and she had to step out from the party and she cried aloud . The very next day she was with me at my home.

Next call was to my eldest sister , she is very down to earth ,not much aware of the tam jhams of the world , and God loving person, she said "Nothing will happen to you, Baba* is going to take care of you .

The next call was to my in-laws, they were also shocked. I still remember my father in law (we lost him in March 2015) saying "Kuch nahi hoga beta" (Nothing will happen to u.)

The series of calls continued, messages floated, from one friend to other, one relative to other, from one person to other and it continued.

Whoever heard the news was shocked, rather few of my close ones / friends asked me not to play a prank on them as April is already over.

But to see the positive side of it not even a single person told me anything negative,

.... all good wishes for a healthy life,

...................get well soon wishes,

..................."we are there and you are always there in our prayers"

.... nothing can happen to you

all such wishes though at that moment didn't go into my ears but today when I sit back and think ,I feel I am here because of all the blessings and those good wishes. As is it said " count your blessings" , and its only because of the

---

* Baba-She use to follow Brahma Kumaris so she mentioned about Brahma Baba and the supreme of all Shiv Baba

blessings and prayers and good wishes that I could come out of it and stand out and shout aloud

"YES I AM A SURVIVOUR"

Yet another difficult night, we were just waiting for the night to get over as the next day we would visit the doctor to know the next course of action, which certainly would be nothing, but to get admitted in the hospital and start the treatment.

"Time and health are two precious assets that we don't recognize and appreciate until they have been depleted"

Denis Waitley

CHAPTER 4
At Office

"The Working lady was no longer a contradiction in terms but a new social phenomenon, emblematic of rapid developments."

Emma Liggins

"If your shoes refuse to shine and your legs don't walk in line and tomorrow is just some other time . That's just the women working on you."

Celine Dion

I had another life too, of a working women ...the news had to be informed at my office too. Definitely not a great news to be shared. Since all this happened just after our appraisals at our office, probably that's the reason my boss didn't respond to my call thinking that it would be a call from me to blow out my frustration. I left a message and then I spoke to my super boss, who was very concerned and gave his support.

The HR was informed, and then a mail floated to the entire employee base of my city, as that's the protocol to be followed .

And it was overwhelming to see the responses after I was admitted in the hospital people coming to the hospital, even those whom I didn't know, people offering prayers and bringing the prashadam for me, people ready to donate their blood, platelets, people calling my husband to know my well being extending their hand to give any support required

HR visits , colleagues visits , and also my boss who had supported to the core throughout the long phase.

Here I would want to mention some funny moments also .

Since the mail had been floated for donating platelets, many people came to the hospital to do so, unknowing the difference between platelets and blood .

A colleague ,who was all in his good health and also hefty and stout , he came for donating platelet ,but was sent back since the lab people could not find the platelets with the correct count , to which this colleague was very annoyed and latter called me and told me " **arey main to ekdum fit hun aur mujhe hospital walon ne bola ki platelet nai le sakte " and he felt very bad   the way he had narrated made me laugh so much. ☺

And this way few other healthy colleagues also could not donate platelets.

Another colleague of mine when he was told by the hospital lab staff that the platelets couldn't be found so he latter told me that he donated his blood "*** hospital donate karne aaya hun, platelet nai to kya hua blood hi donate kar deta hun " ☺

My doctor was also so happy to see the response from my office , he told me in one of the visits that " a full bus filled with people had come from your office to donate "

My Dr. Vaswani use to make me laugh with his positive and kind nature , which use to bring the positive vibrations in the room , and I use to tell him also dr please visit more frequently

"It is not enough to help the feeble up , but to support them after."

WIllian Shakespeare

**I am completely fit still the hospital staff said the platelets couldn't be found.
***I have come to the hospital for donating, if not platelets then at least blood.

CHAPTER 5

The Journey At the Hospital Begins

And the next day we were at the hospital again, to visit the doctor to know my future if its life or death awaiting at the corridor. To be frank no thoughts were there in my mind at that moment, I will live, I will die, what my husband will do after me, what will happen to my daughter who would take care of her etc etc.

After a long wait finally my name was called and I entered the doctors cabin. My doctor (a saviour/GOD/ GOD's angel) tried to comfort me with good words and hopes of my living in this world. He said that the disease CANCER is not good but the one which I have been detected is one of the best ones and to make me laugh he said that in their college while their MBBS study they use to call it the best CANCER, as it is curabale. Ofcourse I could not stop my tears. He called the nurse to start the process of admission ...and the hospital journey began.

Soon the ward boy was there with a wheel chair, I was taken to gynecologist for normal checkup and she found me anemic .... {ahhhh me an anemic...(let me tell you I have been healthy all the while and pretty on the heavier side post my delivery – and just a funny incident when the news broke out to my immediate boss at office the first reaction "you were all healthy and fine till the last day :)} was with my looks and said that I have to be taken in the wheel chair. I was adamant that I could walk to the room but they were not at all confident (probably must be thinking if I fall on some other patient then the poor patient instead of getting treated for the main ailment would first have to be treated for getting crushed below me).☺

The moment I was out of the room I saw my friends standing....true when it is said "that angels do exist, but the ones who do not have wings are called FRIENDS" and yes the same stands true for Sisters also.

They tried to cheer me up....with all the possible ways they could and finally I had a smile on my face. My sisy was standing next to me and my hubby too. The nurse said "patient ko le kar aao"....noooooooooooo not a patient plssss and "I mentioned it to her ...please don't call me patient I have a nice name" at least for the number of days I stay here call me by my name and I must appreciate the staff, they were very good and they followed the same at least in front of me.

As I was entering the room my heart beat was "jhunkkk" it was never so crazy, never ever happened not even when we use to go to take the results of our class examination. All my friends entered the room and my sisy, we all were simply sitting and talking though each one would have their own thoughts .... and then the twist - there came the head nurse (similar to the warden of the hostel) and said "no body is allowed in the room except "Mrs. Kapoor" and one attendant", the room is sterilized hence please go out... and that was the last day that any visitor was allowed in the room.

A big notice with BOLD letters was put on the door "NO VISITORS, NO FLOWERS, NO FRUIT allowed inside" booohhhhh.... And my isolation started.

"The worst cruelty that can be inflicted on a human being is isolation."

Sukarno

CHAPTER 6

Inside The Room

The so called sterlised room (as said by the Head nurse) ---ahhhh it was not at all good feeling to be left alone.

Actually I don't understand how can they tag it to be sterlised, when the doctor who has seen so many patients and the nurses also are all allowed in the room. Big question?

My hubby opted to be the permanent attendant with me in the room.

Today if I imagine it would have been great we 2 being in the room alone, but inside the room there were four walls, one on each side, a oxygen cylinder and many more pipes which was not very soothing to eyes. A table which had a tray with a whole lot of medicines and injections .

The best part in the surrounding was a small window which opened to a church (with a big cross) and the main road.

I use to stand near the window to see the mad rush of people from morning to late evening, vehicles moving and everybody busy in their own schedules leading a crazy life "which ofcourse few days back I was a part of".

A television which was actually an idiot box for me now as I was not even supposed to touch the remote. Side table with newspaper which was as good as put in the trash as I was not supposed to touch it either.

Two beds side by side.

A rod to hold the sline, "could have been used for pole dance if it was fixed :)" and a table with medicines which would soon be a part of my daily doses for the coming few days and a fan which I use to stare at times, thinking why the time doesn't fly as fast as the wings of the fan.

The AC which use to make me shiver but at times I use to think seeing it why the medication is not as noiseless and painless as the AC.

Oh yeah another irritating thing the face mask and the sanitizers (both of which I hated) which would be a part of me till the treatment ends, ofcourse that was not to end soon and take minimum 2 years. The smell of the santizers was so yucky and the face mask made me look so like an alien.

Remembering about the face mask and santizers today after almost 11 years, never had anybody though of these two things being a part of everybody's life, rather an essential, ever since the COVID times have started.

You know I use feel very irritated wearing a face mask and use to question my god, why on this earth I have to use this mask, ofcourse that was for my protection against the infections which I was prone to due to heavy medication. Never the less I knew that from 2020 every one will have to essentially use the mask and sanitizers.

"Solitude, isolation, are painful things and beyond human endurance".

Jules Verne

"We are healed of a suffering only by experiencing it to the full."

Marcel Proust

CHAPTER 7

Fight For A Life Along With Medicines

The treatment had to start the same day and it wasn't too late when the nurse came with a tray with lots of medicines, injections (which I have been fearful always) etc....

And it started ....the journey of poking and prodding, pills, medicine smell all around was never pleasing

The pre chemo medication started and, ofcourse not to mention it was not so good. Nurses visiting every half an hour, checking the temperature, Blood pressure, with a list of dos and don't's.

It was reinforced that the journey would not be an easy one, majorly because no visitor was allowed inside the room except the nurses and doctors and at the same time we were not allowed to step out of the room. It was like an imprisonment, in the right words as put by the doctors "to stay in isolation". In order to stay away from infections. Lot of medicines and the side effect of the medicines, long journey for a term of almost 2 years, giving away of many food items etc etc.

These things although bring a lot of gloominess but at the same time I guess it was for my good hence I had to go through it and majorly as it was the Karma* probably as it is said in Brahma Kumari.

Almost 25-35 pills, 4-5 pokes (injections) and so many times the checking of blood pressure, temperature, heart beat, pulse and other tests. The day use to start with a blood test early morning at 6:00 am.

Then started the first chemo in the evening, people say that they don't believe GOD, I wasn't an atheist, and

*Karma—doings of the past for which the human has to repay in his current birth

GOD's presence was felt through various ways.

First sign of GOD's blessing - The chemo medicine (Liquid) was red in colour and by the time it was getting over gradually it formed a shape of trishool or a cross** which I used to see every day and night at the top of the church which was just next to my hospital. It was a miracle or the faith which showed the existence of GOD, or may be the God himself . Lot of prayers and blessing were there with me and this was definitely not a coincidence but for sure a prodigy.

As I mentioned there was a huge church which was visible from my window. After the chemo I could see the cross light sparkling bright, throwing its light on me and a reassurance by the Lord, a positivity for a fantastic healthy and fit future ahead.

And believe me, this was a good omen and here all doubts end and a new ray of hope is seen. For me I was above all religions at this moment - no Hindu, no Sikh, no Christian, no Muslim - NO RELIGION but a child of the GOD. I have always been a firm believer that "GOD IS ONE and has many names", there were prayers for me from people belonging to all the different religions.

My friends, family from different religions were sending prayers for me, Buddhist chants, my husband's pastor friend were sending healing prayers, the muslim friends were sending their ayaats, Sikhs were sending ardaas and everyone had showered me with their blessings and prayers.

"You just gotta keep going and fighting for everything, and one day you'll get to where you want."

Naomi Osaka

**Trishool—Shivji /Lord Shiva's weapon with three small rods pointing up. Cross of a Jesus

CHAPTER 8

21 Days Journey of Discomforts and Comforts

The second day started when I was injected with one chemo the last day, and so did the after effects of the medicine..."pretty fast ..hummmmnnnn" Nauseating feeling, little bit of weakness, lightheadedness, pulsating feeling in the head, headache, insomnia, and above all a big time foodie like me had gone on a hunger strike...ahhhhh (can never ever imagine me being on a hunger strike). I remember in my childhood I use to skip dinner, since I use to eat a lot of junk in the evening, but there was thumb rule laid by my dad, all have to be at the dinner table and having food together is must.

Well all I wanted to eat always, was my doctors's head with narrating all these expereinces again and again whenever he visited my room. Sudden hunger pangs were there where I wanted to eat all junk which was completely restricted rather a poison for me at that point of time.

Things were very difficult for me as I was not allowed to use a laptop (not for the harmful rays for sure), mobile, no newspaper, not even the remote of the TV, it was all to avoid any infection coming along with these things ahhhhh !!!"Imagine "

There were thousand knocks on the door with so many visitors but all of them were just allowed to wave from outside the door and I lay /sat on the bed inside the room . Visits of so many of them left tears in my eyes. Couldn't even hug my own people who had come over to see me from so far and believe me its not at all easy when you are just few steps away from your loved ones. A hug has always been a remedy , soothing and magical both in happiness and in grief , but what was happening was very very distressing. My sister , my FIL , they use to handover the special cooked food for me at the door , so many times I use to feel, just to hug my sister . My dearest Bhabhi visited me all the way from US , but v could just see each other , tears also couldn't be controlled .

Then day 3 , day 4 and it was heart rending for me and for sure it would have been for Mr. Kapoor also.....my little kiddo had started missing me and more over both the parents were not there with her at home , so it would have been difficult for her too. Though I used to talk to her daily but I wanted to see her, touch her, hug her but couldn't call her to the hospital as it might be disturbing for her to see me in that state , and on top of that the kids weren't allowed inside the hospital wards.

The only way I could see her was from far away , my sister had found out a way - my sisy use to get her to the opposite building , and I use to see her from my room window , and at times she use to bring her to the parking lot which was visible from my room , tears and tears were rolling down my cheeks when I saw her after 5 days.

It is very difficult to control the emotions , especially in such difficult times

Apart from the other side effects of chemo , one of the major side effect of the chemo was losing hair. So I had also started shedding my hair, didn't know that it would start from the 5th day itself . On the pillow I had a a clump of hair and when I told the doc , casually he said that its common, "aisa karo aap baal chote karwa lo" (get your hair short) . Its easy to say but Its tough overall , even though when one knows the fact is that this is all for a new life and betterment of oneself , but the cost is challenging for a girl - without the beautiful hair. . I did not have very long long hair but long enough and it was very painful to see the clump of hair on the pillow, lot of hair strands while washing the hair, while combing the hair .

The strength in these circumstances use to be the blessings and prayers of all my loved ones for my speedy recovery

The journey seemed to be a very long one, no body was telling me as to how many days I would have to stay there, and above all the house arrest in the room of the hospital where I could do nothing but gaze around with a blank mind .

7 Days passed , chemo , medicines, injections , daily reports ,and side effects were very strenuous and were killing me and the seventh day "as in all hindus seven pheras"☺ proved to be a lucky one - the report came as "NILL PROMYLETIOC CELLS" — means the cancer cells were not to be seen in my blood. Hurrraaaahhhhh

A SIGH OF RELIEF AND JOY AND HAPPINESS but it did not mean an end to the daily routine of medication . Still the medicines continued with 20-25 pills on a daily basis , the side effects which were non bearable , the sleeplessness , the ajeebo garib feelings and so many things which is unimaginable and unexplainable

Each day those nurses use to take away so much blood for the daily tests , but the relief use to be seeing the " No cancer cells " in the daily report

I had shed lot of weight (ofcourse had never thought of loosing this way) but guess the good part ☺ that I weighed a few kilos less , along with it I had lost the appetite and my beautiful hair too ☹

Days passed by counting each day , with the hope of getting discharged soon from the hospital and go back to my own home.

Finally day 20th the doc told that I can go home , my own home .

Day 21 , the discharge summary was prepared and it took almost half a day for the formalities to get completed before I could step out of the hospital .

Ofcourse an amazing feeling of getting discharged from the Hospital, but no never the less I knew that from hospital room arrest it would be house room arrest. Looking at the brighter side was that I would be atleast be comfortable at my own house, my own room, my own bed, my own washroom and above all seeing my daughter daily whenever I wanted from near

"Our whole life is set up in the path of least resistance. We don't want to suffer. We don't want to feel discomfort. So the whole time, we're living our lives in a very comfortable area . There's no growth in that."

David Goggins

CHAPTER 9

New Birth With a New Hope and New Life

"Hope is being able to see that there is light despite all of the darkenss."

Desmond Tutu

Yipppeeee ………………………………… the feeling of going home was incredible

Stepping out of the room after 21 days being in isolation , away from everything , Never the less we knew that we would experience this , the legs were jammed not moving and shivering , the heart beats throbbing , seeing the human beings / new faces ,I was feeling they are from a different planet or may be I am an alien .

Since my legs were trembling I was again on a wheel chair ☹

My own people , my near ones waiting for me at home and at the door of the hospital , and in the jiggery wiggery jam , bright light away from the room which had 4 falls , the noise , the traffic , the pollution , the people running around , was making me feel so different - don't know disturbing or happy, but surely I had begun to be back into this beautiful world

I finally reached home , my home, my room ,my bed , my people ,my daughter ………………Astounding

"Where we live is home-home that our feet may leave, but not our hearts ."

Oliver Wendell Holmes, Sr.

But as there is a twist in all the live/ reality games/shows shown on the television , for me too it was - i was still to be under the house arrest or to say in isolation , stay away from people (as people do carry infections) , believe me I had to stay away from my daughter too . Though my own home but lot of restrictions, along with no meeting people, no eating stale food , no outside food, no packed food/snacks , no raw food, no fruits and only no , no and no for all the things which makes one feel so unlively.

The ardous thing for me was the face mask which I had to put on always while awake.

At the same time the solace of being in my own zone - "my own home " and my own people around and also no more injections, checks and test for few more days .

0p6.4 However the oral chemo along with other medicines (precisely 22 pills a day) , the struggle with oneself and the after effects of the medicines continued

The news had spread like fire in our apartment and neighborhood, and if by chance they found me near the window or the door , I swear their inquisitiveness by their looks use to be more horrifying than my disease... a sympathetic look , or investigating looks ,as if its so dreadful and along with it a list of instructions (as if they were the doctor) . People's such behavior at times is not acceptable during such situations .

I would like to add here very strongly that in case if we come across anybody who is suffering from any kind of disease one should be empathetic instead of sympathetic, as it really bothers the person suffering , the doctor is doing their job and let the person suffering take good care of themselves.

Doctors do not reveal many things to the patients , probably cause that might concern the patient and would cause stress ,but I guess they should atleast tell the good things. The house arrest for me had to be there for 15 days and the doctor didnt mention, Even though being in my house, but staying in the room locked throughout the day and night was really dishearenting and uncomfortable and irritating and suffocating and I can actually write down so many synonyms .buuuuuuurrrrrrrrrrrr !!!!!!!!!!!!!!

I use to step out only when there was no one at home , I was served the food from the door as no one was supposed to step into my room , and now it was only me and my room .Yeah , I had the levy of watching the TV and working on the laptop (can you believe it that all these items were cleaned with a cotton ball dipped in detol eehhhhhhh always detoly smell), but at atleast I could use them , most of the time I used to surf on cancer survivor stories , which use to make me strong mentally and emotionally.

Use to talk in between with my kiddo who use to stand near the door, the thought itself brings shivers to me , a small girl of 3 years , traumatic for her too.

My sister , my husband , my mom , my inlaws all use to be outside the room , and I use to hear their voices from inside. I wanted to just bang open the door and step out of the room and sit with all of them , talk, but the reality was just to stay inside and keep listening

Not being a part of the conversation, It was too tormenting

"Family is not an important thing , it's everything."
Michael J Fox

"We must accept finite disappointment , but never lose infinite hope."
Martin Luther King . Jr.

CHAPTER 10

Second Visit to the Hospital

Although the doctor prescribed three rounds/cycle of chemo but being fearful to go through the pain again , I use to pray an end to it. My innocence of mistaking things.

I was mentally preparing my self for the Second chemo to face the injections and side effects , and it was not too late when I had to visit the hospital again to start the second round of Chemo.

Again the same room, nurses, hospital , medicine smell, hospital bed and the torture for good started.

This time I had become a little week both ,physically - internally and externally and mentally too

The side effects of the chemo were more prominently experienced by me, my God and prayers were the only two strong things which had kept me up and live ,a nd the support of my husband, sisters and family members.

Thankfully this time it was not an imprisonment in the hospital for 21 days and ended in 5 days (a sigh of relief). But yes ofcourse the house imprisonment was again for 15 days post return from the hospital.

These 5 days have been horrendous , as after the first day chemo I just lay on the bed and use to be sleepy always . Same medication , same prodding and poking, and test as I said earlier the solace was : no cancer cells visible " in the reports .

The effects were prominently visible and experienced, stomach ache, nausea, hair fall, cranky feeling, lightheadedness , throbbing near the ear .

You know the most treacherous part is the canuala which is injected on the patients hand as soon as the person is admitted in the hospital...I just wish that there should be some invention that the same should be eradicated .

Finally the five days were over and again my discharge summary was prepared and I was allowed to step out .Thankfully no more cramps in the legs , but the weekness prevailed.

As they say that chemo not only destroys the bad cells but also the good cells , which was visible clearly . the body had become weak, and was not ready to take the medication as strongly as in the first chemo cycle. But the thought that it was for a good and healthy future , was taking all this as it was coming .

Back on the way home same feelings of being an alien where I had to put the face mask , whereas the other people around could move freely , I swear the looks given by other people when they saw me in the mask was so annoying .

The 5 days of isolation to be converted into another 15 days of isolation at home

"Positive feelings come from being honest about yourself and accepting your personality , and physical characteristics , warts and all , and from belonging to a family that accepts you without question."

Willard Scott

Chapter 11

The Hair Story

"A women who cuts her hair is about to change her life."

salonbusiness.com

The other side effects were ofcourse very griming , along with the hairfall.

I finally had to decide of either letting the hair fall here and there daily in clumps each time I comb or sleep on the bed or else just chop them off/or to elegantly state it hairdo☺

Since house arrest followed hence could not go the salon hence made an alternate to cut the long hair myself. Onerous ....yes !!!!!!

All set – a pair of scissors, comb, mirror, sprinkler and me – the new hair stylist ..... ha ha ☺

Stood in front of the mirror , and there my hairstylist instincts were on its high as a women paralley a patient for the self my hands were trembling ,rather I was trembling.....

I just stood and looking at my hair , in two minds again, deciding on to what length should I cut them , will it grow back soon , what will be the reaction from my kiddo seeing me in short hair , what will my husband say, will he like me in this new hairdo , and so many thoughts ...rather a wave of thoughts.

However ,with some courage from my baba just held the strands and started cutting and it started dropping on the floor ......I stood motionless there seeing the hair lying on the floor....had cut them too short, above the shoulder, almost touching the ears.

After a moment , when I realized , I could just scream on top of my voice aloud and aloud......cried and cried and cried and cried

Kind of a melodrama - indeed (but as said correctly it is difficult)

My sister for whom I am like her child , she heard my scream and got tensed , she started banging my room door , but since I was crying and locked in the restroom, I didn't realize .

She was so tensed that she came out of the house to peep from the window, but the window was also closed, and she knocked the window too....All went for almost 10 minutes , after which I opened the door and hugged her from far and we both were in tears.

At last she said no worries , it would grow back again

The good part was the hair fall was now not prominently visible , as I had almost shed a major chunk and remaining I had chopped

Evening when he saw me , I could feel he was also tensed that all hair is gone and then I narrated the entire story of the afternoon , to which he also reacted very calmly and jokingly " wow looking beautiful in the new hairstyle , do keep short hair once it regrows "

My kiddo couldn't stop her laughter seeing me in short hair. I was happy that it is bringing smile on her face.

In all this daily episodes ,which I never realized at that point of time but today while narrating this to you all, I really feel bad for my mom. She would be having so many questions in her mind and also it would be so traumatic for her to see her own child suffering . We had never shared with her that I was suffering from cancer due to her age and had just said that it is due to some infection in the body. Today she is no more and after my treatment never had the chance or I should better say that never had the courage to ask her if she knew the reality of my sufferings.

To my mom :- where ever you are today , I am sorry for not telling you the reality ,but for us you were important and didn't want you to undergo any kind of mental stress .

I remember my mother's prayers and they have always followed me. They have clung to me all my life.

Chapter 12

Passing Days

Days passed , with both negative and positive thoughts in my mind , discussions / conversations with my family — sister, daughter , husband ,in laws, mom from two separate rooms.

Finally 15 days isolation was over and I was allowed to move within the house. Weakness, the feeling of the emptiness was prevailing strongly but I had to keep myself lively for my own people.

Everyday seemed to be one long day, when I use to peep out of the window /or stand in the balcony and see people moving around freely without any hesitation/ restriction , I used to consider them to be lucky.

Facts of life - we realize the worth of things and people, when we face difficulties , or when we are not content.

By this time my state was like an injured bird who has been imprisoned not only to fly , but also to eat , drink , talk . Had Lost most of the stamina .

Since rains had started I used to feel more gloomy, as I couldn't go out to get drenched in the rain (my favorites during rains). This season brings lot of infections and viruses along with it and at times i use to be infected with cold and cough. My hemoglobin had reduced drastically and all measures were being taken to stabilize .

With a week body I had to prepare myself for the third and most likely and hopefully the last cycle of chemo , which would start at the end of 30 days

"As long as there is a new twist in the storyline, there cannot be any space for monotony."

Divyanka Tripathi

CHAPTER 13

Last Stay at the hospital

"You don't appreciate life until you get to the other side. Like lying in a hospital bed."

Fabrice Muamba

Third and last chemo , same procedure — getting admitted, sterilized room, medicine smell all around and one more smell which even today irritates me to the core : the so called sanitizer), poking and prodding - the poking and prodding had become a kind of my destiny " ab to shayad dard ka ehsaas hi nai hota tha ya phir itni baar ye suiyaan chubh chuki thi ki adaat si ho gai thi "

This time even more agonizing ,even more feeble, even more tough, even more severe , even more side effects .

Again a five day stay, but this time a more demanding one.

The first day itself made me feel so week . Was not able to step down of the bed even. Each day the side effects were higher and higher getting more and more worse .

The fifth day was finally there and it was the last chemo for me and I was very cheerful only in thoughts , as now there would be good and painless days

Less to be aware that although the prodding chemo is over but there is a long way to go , indeed a prolonged one.

The doctor informed that I have to be on medication - oral chemo for 2 years and also isolation has to be maintained ,although not in a room but had to avoid all public places , crowded places as the side effects of the oral chemo would result in low immunity

Low immunity would in turn make me prone to infections and the most difficult part is to be cautious and alert was , to save one self from the infection or getting infected from the atmosphere/ air , people around , season etc etc and a never ending etc.

Another journey to begin a loooonnngggg one and a painful one indeed. since I was more week and more prone to the infections , with the changing season worse things were in store for me.

As said that the bad things long last and good things get over soon , was so much relevant to me.

Again was under a house arrest of 21 days and once the days were over it was movement only inside the house.

Difficult to follow, difficult to describe by putting it merely in words

With the changing season was not aware what is in store for me , and then things detoriated

Due to the changing season, rainy season on its peak in the month of August the worst of all had to happen.Cold and cough started - one which lasted for almost 2 months (longest in my life ever) with lot - of negative thoughts and irritation . But less I knew that the these intermittent gaps of not taking the chemo medicine would actually increase my time from 2 years plus the number of days /gaps

Was I really so bad , or have I done such bad deeds in life that I had to undergo this process was the thought everytime and due to all these effects my irritation level use to be at its peak.

In order to control the cold and cough which was not ready to leave me , as if it had fallen in love with me , the chemo medication had to be stopped for some time so that the immunity becomes stronger and the body recovers faster from the normal flu . Not only cold cough but with it accompanied low hemoglobin levels ,leading to head throbbing always and just could not do anything about it.

...aahhh use to feel so feeble and weak and irritated, as if its just a lifeless body

Long chats with friends , surfing on the net , and complaining to the close buddies had become a regular routine for me.:(

To pen down the journey of two year is not easy job. With each passing day I use to think that good times are gonna start for me. And with every good thing or a positive move or a good news related to my health I used to feel elated

Finally, in one fine visits to the doctor I was told that I can have packed food from the market. As you all know packed food is kinda necessity for most of us .So that evening had *biscuits/packed food. Though it would sound very small thing but believe me it was like winning a lottery.

With each passing day life was becoming both under control and uncontroable , Positive as well as negative .

In this entire process two things which were happening good were that I had started meditating and my belief in GOD (despite of religions) was becoming stronger and also that I had lost lot of weight (ofcourse not the right way of losing — GOD forbid no one should undergo such a process to lose weight)

**Meditation is something which is the entire game plan of the mind . you feel something ,some source to be with you , the power around you, the soul is always protecting you and giving energy .A rays of positiveness which touches your heart your soul your body your mind and your feelings...a complete esctacy

I had felt all the gods near me , visitng me at my home , during the chemo sitting next to me ,...may be it is just my feelings or thoughts but as it is said to believe one has to experience and I had experienced it all

I was due for one bone marrow test just for a reconfirmation that the medicine has worked for me .

The test as mentioned earlier (bone marrow) is one of the most painful test and I was scared of the entire pricking again. But believe me , I was just remembering my BABA (one supreme soul) and during the entire process of the test I could feel he is sittng next to me and I did not feel even a pinch of the test pain...as I said earlier one has to experience these all things to believe it.

Chapter 14

The Biscuit Story

"I have the simplest tastes. I am always satisfied with the best."

Oscar Wilde

Not the story of any biscuit , but as I mentioned in the last chapter it is about me eating the biscuit.

Right from the day the treatment for the blood cancer : Acute Promylotic Cancer " had started there were lot of restrictions imposed (as I had mentioned in earlier chapters) ,similar restriction was imposed on my food intake . Strict no to raw food , stale food and packaged or ready to eat food

In the last visit the doctor said I can consume ready to eat food and packaged food , so as with the evening tea the mixtures and biscuits are a must , one evening since I was allowed to move freely in the house atleast, while having the evening tea , I was served the packet of biscuit ,along with the evening tea.

OMG I was so elated

And imagine which biscuits ..My favourite " Parle G "

Vo biscuit aur unko vo chai main dubo dubbo kar khana , (Dip the biscuit in the tea and eat) believe me it was like being in heaven.

I had never felt the taste so good ever before, was having after almost 4 months

And also I think I would have never chewed it for such a long time , and enjoying ....., perfect pleasure

Sounds a very small thing , but that evening I felt that my life of leading it like an alien has stopped and is back into the normal human being life .

Yes, I remember and many a times I still see the picture clicked by my hubby. I had turned bad, half hair , lean, black and no charm on the face ,but with the hope of becoming the same beautiful girl I was , my fight continued.

Today I sit back and think , then it would be a nice idea for promotion of biscuits for Parle – G

"There is no sincerer love than the love of food."

George Bernard Shaw

Chapter 15

Journey Begins — 2 years

The 3 time stay at hospital was over, which was indeed a big relief for me .

"Its been a long , painful journey, with lots of comforts and discomforts, from where I started to where I am today Cured and I feel blessed with God's Grace, but another long journey to go. ....and I am all ready ....."

That has passed ...and this shall also pass.

Kavita Passi

Doctor had clearly told that the journey is long since the medication is for 2 years and in case if due to some reason the medicine is stopped in between the time from two years would increase to the the number of gaps in between .

The oral chemo medicines were continued, so did the regular check ups after every 15 days and visitng the doctor with the reports. The relief was when all the parameters in the report use to give the correct reading . The isolation continued but yes it was not bound within the four walls , but within the house or on the terrace or to places where no one visits /no crowded places

The mask was a regular feature everytime I stepped out of the house since is was still not ready to leave me , and ofcourse the few restrictions continued.

But I fought each day and felt I am nearing to recovery and Victory

Lot of things good and bad happened with me , for me in these years. Lets take it one by one.

Chapter 16

1 Year of Survival

"It takes but one positive thought when given a chance to survive and thrive to overpower an entire army of negative thoughts."

Robert H. Schuller

One year passed , and it called for a celebration. Just a year before the disease was diagnosed and , today I was categorized as the Cancer Survivor. Great achievement yeaaaahhhhh...... Free of Cancer. Though after the third chemo itself the cancer cells were thankfully out of my body but yes a year is a long period . 365 days equivalent to may be 365 into infinity. Very difficult. Very strenous , very irritating , very long

But as it is said "All is well that ends well ", though the journey of another year was still there and the fight had to continue but yes I was now a survivor and that was more important for me and probably for all my near and dear ones as well as my family and friends

By this time I had become a part of many survivor groups online, and twice I was called for sharing my experience too .

My onco was very happy with my positivity and wanted me to be an example and in many visits of regular checkups he used to introduce me to the patients before me and after me (in sequence) and set me as an example of a true fighter.

I, while in the wait time of my turn at the lobby of the

hospital used to interact with few patients . Seeing their faces it was quite obvious that they were unaware of what will happen next, and in such scenarios only negative thoughts prevails in the mind ,they seemed to be really scared who had been just detected recently ,unaware of the pros and cons of the treatment,

After our conversation, I used to feel the difference in their attitude, and I used to feel good that my words could comfort them a little .

I use to tell my doc , that he should appoint me as the counsellor ☺

Many used to ask for my number, I never hesitated in sharing the same, and there were many who use to call me to ask me so many things.

"Life is the only counselor , wisdom unfiltered through personal experience does not become a part of the the moral tissue."

Edith Wharton

Chapter 17

Peak of Uncertainty — Testing times

"Anyway, no drug, not even alcohol, causes the fundamental ills of society, if we're looking for the source of our troubles, we shouldn't test people for drugs, we should test them for stupidity , ignorance , greed and love of power."

P.J,O'Rourke

When in difficult times , testing times the person gives up the patience also .

Regular check up , regular doctor visits, all preacutions and restrictions being followed as prescribed , but in one of the visits , I had totally given up .

Morning as scheduled went to the hospital along with my husband, gave the blood sample for the regular tests as prescribed , and after almost an hour came back for the reports , seeing the report the doctor was also dumb struck , how can the reports again go hay wire .

With a very heavy heart he said that , the cells are showing active... I still remember I just stood up from the table, on one side was the doctor and on the other side was my hubby , inside the doctors chamber.

I clearly told the doctor , I do not want any more medication, if this is my fate so be it ...please stop my treatment and if God has decided this for me then may be there is some good in it.

I will stop all medication , I will stop all tests, I will stop all precautions. Enough of everything .

He was trying to compose me , that sometimes it happens but we will come out off it , but I was adamant this time, I said no I would not go further for any more treatments .

My hubby also tried to compose me but I was totally a different person that point of time .

Then the doctor said, to give some more time to him , and I should come back after 2 hours.

In a rage of anger I banged the door and stepped out of the room. Mr. Kapoor tried to calm me down , and then we drove to a nearby church (remember I had mentioned in the first chapters that I use to see a church from the window of the hospital room)

Both of us sat inside the church for almost more than an hour with folded hands, prayed and prayed. (on every visit to the doctor I use to ensure that we go the church also)

"Faith is to believe what you do not see , the reward of this faith is to see what you believe."

Saint Augustine

When we came back to the hospital almost after 2 hours and entered the doctors chamber he had a smile on his face, as if he has also been relieved of some big tension .

He said nothing to worry , there was a glitch by the technician , he (doc) himself went to the lab sat with the technician and checked the sample again and the glitch was just a 0 added to the WBC* figure while typing .

I think the prayers were heard and it was proven that prayers can do wonders and miracles.

---

*WBC- white blood cells, the reading was mistakenly given as 14000 instead of 1400.

Me and Mr.Kapoor both took a sign of relief and so did the doc.

We came back home, but this incident had left us shaken. Just a small error can be of so much of pain.

"Even a happy life cannot be without a measure of darkness , and the word happy would lose its meaning if it were not balanced by sadness. It is far betterto take things as they come along with patience and equanimity."

Carl Jung

Chapter 18

Media Attention

I was called for sharing my experience at different places , getting attention by the print media , media actually gave me a boost , but ofcourse had never thought that I would have to voive for such a trechorous disease.

But as it is said , GOD makes his chosen people for good work , and suffering and going through , I would be glad if I can be of any help to anyone on this beautiful earth.

One doctors summit conducted by Dr. Reddy's , especially for oncologists and the other on the World Cancer Day at the hospital where I was treated .

And print media - One newpaper (TOI) also had my interview printed on the paper on the World Cancer Day

It felt good and gradually I had the thought of helping or counselling people and families who were undergoing the same thing

Dr. Reddy's — One of the renowned pharma company had organized a doctors summit in one of the big hotels in my city , where lot of doctors were invited

I was excited as well as nervous to narrate my story / experiences in front of more than 500 people , but I felt that the doctors should know what a patient undergoes through the treatment .

I started preparing the speech , a long one which had to be cut short but at the same time had to cover almost everything.

I will share my speech with you all here :-

Similar to the one mentioned in the chapter

The next speech was to be given at the hospital on the World Cancer Day – I was smart enough so I repeated the same speech with a little bit of tweaking .

The coverage was huge, the print media as well as the social media were there with their cameras and mikes . Few interviews were taken .

My interview glimpse was aired on the social media and I literally called so many people to watch the same , since it was on a regional channel many did not have the access , but I viewed it myself and made a video of the same and shared with my family and friends

And then one of the Print media – "Times of India" *published my interview, though I kept my name anonymous

---

*Published on : Date 04.02.2016 on the World Cancer Day.

WE CAN. I CAN, DEFEAT CANCER

The World Cancer Day theme of We Can. I Can, emphasizes a collective approach to beat cancer. What's important is to provide support to cancer patients so that they regain their confidence

Megha.Deshpande
@timesgroup.com

Every year February 4 is observed as the World Cancer Day. The aim of this day's observance is to unite people from all walks of life across the globe, to fight against this ailment. Currently cardiac arrest is the first major cause of mortality across the globe and it is estimated that if cancer goes unchecked then it might take the top slot of mortality cause by 2025. The Union for International Cancer Control, which is based in Geneva, along with its 800 member organisations across 155 countries, spearheads various activities pertaining to awareness, treatment and other related aspects of cancer. Doctors unanimously emphasize that cancer, if diagnosed early, is curable. Certain lifestyle discipline and regular medical check-up is all that is needed to begin with.

'We Can. I Can,' is the theme for the World Cancer Day this year. This theme will extend till 2018. As the theme title goes, it's just not the patient, but everybody else directly and indirectly associated with him or her, needs to be pro-active in the fight against cancer. "When a person is told that he is diagnosed with cancer, he generally goes blank. Once it sinks in then all sorts of thoughts pop up. However for fighting cancer what's

important is to have faith as it helps in building immense will power," says Kavita, a cancer survivor who now devotes considerable time for counselling cancer patients.

While genetic pre-disposition determines whether one is prone to develop cancer or not, even lifestyle habits or rather wrong habits contribute to one's risk of developing this malignancy. Consumption of tobacco, *gutka*, alcohol and cigarette smoking increase the risk of developing cancer, opine medical practitioners. "In India men are prone to either oral cavity cancer or lung cancer which can be easily correlated to consumption of tobacco, *gutka* and cigarette smoking," says Dr Bharat Vaswani, senior oncologist, Yashoda Hospitals. "Breast cancer, cervical cancer and ovarian cancer affect women. If there is no cancer history in the family then from the age of 35 women must go for screen

tests and in case there is a family history then at 30 itself these tests must be regularly done," says Dr Vaswani.

Without any exception one must eat fresh fruits and regularly exercise. Quitting smoking reduces the risk of cancer by 50 per cent over the following 10 years, say medical practitioners. Refraining from consuming any amount of alcohol only helps in maintaining one's health. Equally important is to reach out to patients who are suffering from cancer.

In western countries, cancer patients as well as survivors form groups, extending support to each other. Whereas in India, speaking up about one's experience with cancer is not commonly found. "People must be sensitive and not overly sympathize with cancer patients as that depresses them all the more. Cancer survivors themselves must come out and counsel others who are still suffering from malignancy," says Kavita.

Chapter 19

Second Year of Survival

A year had passed , and another year of the journey was remaining. Actually, though told by the doctor the treatment had to go for a year ,but as I had mentioned earlier there were many gaps when I had to stop taking the oral chemo. At the times when the season changed.

The cold and cough in between, especially during the seasonal change attacked my body and hence I had to stop the medicines in between and as a result the 2 year course got extended by few months actually to be precise 6 months .

From 2011 September to 2014 February — the total period of the oral chemo apart from the first three cycle from 2011 may to 2011 August.

The sufferings due to the side effects had become little less by 10-20 % , the visits to the doctor was prolonged from every 15 days , to every month and finally from every month to every quarter .

My hair had gradually started coming back , the stamina was though low by 70% but I was feeling better now.

The tests continued , restrictions continued , medicines continued , the mask continued but internally I was stronger at the same time weak , and a new name was given to me by my dear ones " Fighter " , " Strong Girl "

This disease, this undergoing of the pain had taught me lot things in life, made lot of changes in my body, emotionally physically and mentally I was a different me.

I started valuing life , started giving more importance

to exercise and yoga was the hope for me

    "I do believe there is heaven . I do believe that God has given me the resilience and the syrvival skills to withstand the chiffon trenches ."

Andre Leon Talley

CHAPTER 20

Vaccation During the Disease

Yes you read it right, vacation. Though everything was restricted but with the permission by my onco was granted for me to go for a short vacation, may be to keep up my spirits high, may be because I had suffered so much and a much needed break was essential for me. Since the doc had said yes to it hence all at home were also ready for the same

And we chose ☺☺ty to be the destination – a small pace, less crowded.

But I was excited, to go out of the city, new place, new people, journey, scenic beauty.

I couldn't believe it myself, when I was at the airport I was feeling so scared to be alone. My hubby and kiddo were there with me, but I felt as if I was travelling for the very first time in life.

My cousins joined us at the Coimbatore airport and finally we reached the ☺☺TY. Lovely place, lovely ambience as expected not much of crowd, but yes my mask was always on as usual.

We visited all the places there, had hundred of pictures clicked some with mask some without mask , those lovely mountains , lakes and the tea gardens and the roads with those coconut trees on both sides of the road . On the way I felt it's the road going to heaven.. I was so elated. Felt the same pleasure as a small child gets when he/she is given a toy in the hand to play. Was feeling as if this is the first trip of my life. So many mixed feelings...totally unexpressable.

I enjoyed the trip thoroughly, experiencing a new life again.

It is rightly said change is the spice of life, after returning I was a new me. Staying indoors for such a long time, I felt I had become very introvert, but after the trip I could feel I am the same rather more confident person all together.

I started having a more positive approach towards everything

"A vacation is what you take when you can no longer take what you've been taking."

Earl Wilson

Chapter 21

Astrology /Palmist

I had never believed on Astrology, numerology, stones, palmistry, although I use to enjoy reading my horoscope column in the newspaper edition every morning, or even in the weekly and monthly magazines , but nothing more than that.

I have seen and known so many people around me who believe in these things so much that every move they take they refer to their guru or palmists .

I remember I was in standard 12th and my sister had taken to one of the palmists to know my future , that palmist asked me to wear 2-3 stones /gems but I refused, to which he got so annoyed and challenged me that the stars are such that if I do not wear the gem stones then it wouldn't be good for me .

Well even though I didn't listen to him and took the things light and believed if I put my bet efforts I will succeed in life.

Well as I said , people around me use to be firm believer of these nakstras and all , and amongst them is my elder sister.

In 2011 , the year I got diagnosed with the disease , I visited her in the month of February ,and agai she took me to another Palmist Mr. Upender at Ranchi,

A nice gentleman and the way he told me , I really felt good that in todays world also there are some palmists who have such in-depth knowledge ,

He took my details and gave some predictions, and advised few things to do .

But as there is a saying , " jo jo jub jub hona hota hai vo ho kar hi rehta hai" (whatever is destined, happens)

The palmist had mentioned year wise major incidents in the writeup (janampatri), we missed out on the major one ...no one read it , neither me , nor my sister , nor my hubby , where as clearly he had written "scope of blood related disease" for which he had advised Pooja also but since we had missed it hence it happened.

Latter Mr. Upender mentioned also that he had already warned us about the disease, ofcourse he also mentioned that I would come out of it also.

From that day onwards I also started believing in this study and lot of respect for them.

Till today everytime I visit Ranchi, I do visit Mr. Upender to check with him if all the stars are in their right house for me

And Mr. Upender, from Dhurva, Ranchi, popularly known as Babu Bhaiya the famous palmist's predictions have always been bang on the mark .

"Maybe palmistry was about reassuring you that your destiny's in your hands."

Lanlocked Sailor

Chapter 22

Meditation and Faith

"I have brought myself, by long meditation, to the conviction that a human being with a settled purpose must accomplish it, and that nothing can resist a will which will stake even existence upon its fulfillment."

Benjamin Disraeli

God is the supreme power, right from our childhood we have been taught by our parents , that God listens to our prayers.

Being brought up in an aethist family , daily morning and evening we use to light the diya in the Pooja ghar at our home and pray,

Regular visits to the temple and gurudwara, along with learning of slokas and mantras and ardas was taught to me by my mother.

I have always been an ardent follower and believer of GOD, though he is one, is what I believe but human mankind has given HIM so many names .

As I had mentioned earlier , many prayers were being done for me by my friends and family and within all these , there came my Mamaji and my elder sister who had been following BRAHMA KUMARIS , the centre was very near to my house so all the sisters and brothers at the Brahma Kumari centre was requested to pray for me.

Once my Chemo cycle was over and I was back home, and out of isolation, special class was arranged for me separately only for me at the centre , by the centre head didi , and from that day I became a part of the BRAHMA KUAMRIS.

With each day my faith in the brahma baba was stronger and stronger and to believe the supreme soul Shiv Baba , who gave me complete strength to fight and come out of the situation . Lot of didi's use to send healing thorugh yog to me for my recovery, and thorugh the mediation process I also learned self healing

During and right from the day I was admitted in the hospital, as I mentioned earlier all my friends and family sent their prayers and good wishes their way .

Reiki is one of the self healing techniques , which was followed by my father , and even both the elder sisters , and my cousins, so Reiki healing was also arranged by one of the grand masters Mr. Mehta at Chandigarh, and I swear I had really troubled him so much. Whenever I use to face any challenge at any given point of time I use to call him and ask him to send healing for me .

After my isolation period was over , after the completion of all the three cycles I also took Reiki classes from one grand master at Hyderabad . And it does work .

Actually the main point is that one should believe it to feel the same , experience it to have faith .

Nutsheel is Believe it - Have complete Faith — feel it and experience the difference

During my stay at the hospital and even after that so many times I had so many dreams where I could feel the showers of blessings by GOD , God visiting our house, Standing at the door , knocking the door, blessing me with his hand on my head.

Many a times I felt Lord Jesus walking in my room to bless me and make me believe that I would come out of it completely

I had even experienced Buddhism with the chant of "Nam Yo Ho Reng Ye Kyo"

And firmly believe...

GOD is one ......

Preachings are one ......

With Different Names , religion , caste .....

"Faith is taking the first step even when you don't see the whole staircase ."

Martin Luther King Jr.

Chapter 23

Life Continues with a Positive Hope and All Faith

Life continues with a positive hope and all faith

Finally the doctor said I am free of the medicines and can have a normal life.

People / relatives till date either on call or when they meet ask me is I am still on medication, which bothers me a lot, enquire about my disease but then that's how people around us are

Few things :-

"Have Faith on HIM

Do not loose hope

Stay strong with your will power

Meditate

Exercise

Eat healthy

Stay positive and happy

Don't let anyones words affect you or make you feel low

Have a happy and healthy and long life

You're braver than you believe and stronger than you seen, and smarter than you think."

A A Mine

CHAPTER 24

Covid Times

The most deadliest phase for human mankind hit the Universe in March 2020 , good bad or Ugly , no one knows , but of course very uncertain and unpredictable nothing has been hidden from any one , but the same reminded me of the Cancer phase coz masking up and sanitizing was an essential for me that time and now it is for everyone.

During this phase lot of people came up with their talents, and I got an opportunity to finish my book . I had started this long back but unfortunately didn't get time to complete the book , rather also during the Covid phase , but when I contracted the disease in the third wave, I could complete the same,

As it is said in Geeta "Jo hota hai Ache ke liye hota hai " whatever happens , happens for good .

So probably I contracted Covid to finish my Book , hence one should be always thankful to GOD

CHAPTER 25
Personal Physical Transformation

Lot of things had changed post medication , and as it is said once the life comes on track people again start taking it for granted.

Although I use to be physically active and exercise but that was not a regular feature , and as a result I had become overweight.

My doctor also use to ask me to reduce the weight but I had never taken it very seriously .

Yes during the Covid times , not only did I started writing my book but also started working on my physical transformation. For sure would try to come up with an edition on the physical transformation , the natural way at home .

Today I stand as a complete new ME

"Physical fitness is not only one of the most important keys to healthy a body , it is the basis of dynamic and creative intellectual activity."

John F. Kennedy